Zoey AND SASSAFRAS

UNICORNS AND GERMS

READ THE REST OF THE SERIES

for activities and more visit
ZOEYANDSASSAFRAS.COM

TABLE OF CONTENTS

FOR NINA NORMA — ML
FOR GOOSE AND BUBS . . . AND BABY NINA! — AC

Audience: Grades K-5.
LCCN 2018905029
ISBN 9781943147465; ISBN 9781943147472; ISBN 9781943147489; ISBN 9781943147496

Text copyright 2018 by Asia Citro
Illustrations copyright 2018 by Marion Lindsay
Journal entries handwritten by S. Citro

Published by The Innovation Press
1001 4th Avenue, Suite 3200 Seattle, WA 98154
www.theinnovationpress.com

Printed and bound by Worzalla
Production Date: May 2018 | Plant Location: Stevens Point, Wisconsin

Cover design by Nicole LaRue | Book layout by Kerry Ellis

PROLOGUE

These days my cat Sassafras and I are always desperately hoping we'll hear our barn doorbell.

I know most people are excited to hear their doorbell ring. It might mean a present or package delivery, or a friend showing up to play. But our doorbell is even more exciting than that. Because it's a *magic* doorbell. When it rings, it means there's a magical animal waiting outside our barn. A magical animal who needs our help.

My mom's been helping them basically her whole life. And now *I* get to help, too ...

CHAPTER 1
MYSTERY PROJECT

I threw open the front door, tossed my backpack to the ground, and scooped up Sassafras.

"I missed you so much!" I kissed his head.

Sassafras licked my nose, then sniffed my ear.

"Yep, it's still better. No more ear infection!" I spun him once, then set him down. I popped my head in the kitchen. "Mooooommm? I'm home!"

No Mom. But there was a bunch of stuff set out on the kitchen counter.

"Mrrowww?" Sassafras asked from the floor.

"Here you go, Sassafras!" I picked him up to give him a better view. Mom had set out a carton of whole milk, a little container of plain yogurt, a bunch of jars, a pot, a big spoon, and a food thermometer. "What could it be for?"

Sassafras touched the milk carton with a paw. "Mrrowww?"

"I didn't hear you come in!" Mom walked into the kitchen. "I thought we could make something new today." Mom came up behind me and put her hands on my shoulders. "Have you figured out what we're making yet?"

"I know it's something with a lot of milk. Wait, is it cheese?"

"Not cheese, but good guess." Mom tapped the little container of yogurt. "We're going to make homemade yogurt!"

Sassafras purred.

"Yum! But wait, we have a container of yogurt there. I don't get it. Are we making yogurt with . . . yogurt?"

"Sort of. Did you know that you only need two ingredients to make homemade yogurt?"

"Really? Just milk and . . . yogurt?"

"In a way, yes! Technically you only need milk and live bacteria. You could order live bacteria online, but it's much easier to get it from store-bought yogurt."

Sassafras growled.

"LIVE bacteria? As in, it's still alive?" I took a step back. "But I just got rid of the bacteria that gave me an ear infection."

Mom laughed and ruffled Sassafras's fur. "There are all kinds of bacteria in and on your body right now."

In and *on* my body? Yeesh. Sassafras puffed up and I set him down to scratch my arms.

Mom laughed harder. "Oh, you two! Only some bacteria are harmful. In fact, most are helpful. Bacteria in your body help you digest food when you eat, they keep your insides safe from dangerous bacteria and viruses, and of course"—Mom made a dramatic wave with her arm—"we even use some kinds of bacteria to make delicious food."

Mom pulled a chair over for Sassafras and nudged the pot, carton of milk, and recipe toward me.

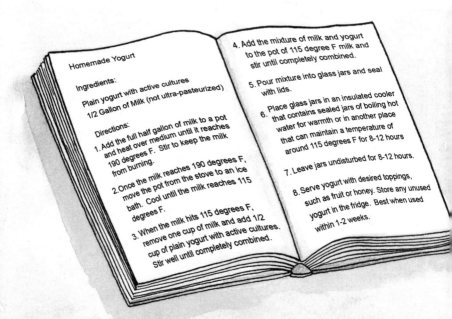

Homemade Yogurt

Ingredients:
Plain yogurt with active cultures
1/2 Gallon of Milk (not ultra-pasteurized)

Directions:
1. Add the full half gallon of milk to a pot and heat over medium until it reaches 190 degrees F. Stir to keep the milk from burning.

2. Once the milk reaches 190 degrees F, move the pot from the stove to an ice bath. Cool until the milk reaches 115 degrees F.

3. When the milk hits 115 degrees F, remove one cup of milk and add 1/2 cup of plain yogurt with active cultures. Stir well until completely combined.

4. Add the mixture of milk and yogurt to the pot of 115 degree F milk and stir until completely combined.

5. Pour mixture into glass jars and seal with lids.

6. Place glass jars in an insulated cooler that contains sealed jars of boiling hot water for warmth or in another place that can maintain a temperature of around 115 degrees F for 8-12 hours

7. Leave jars undisturbed for 8-12 hours.

8. Serve yogurt with desired toppings, such as fruit or honey. Store any unused yogurt in the fridge. Best when used within 1-2 weeks.

Sassafras watched from the chair, and Mom helped me with the steps involving the stove. When we got to the part where I stirred some of the store-bought yogurt into some of the warm milk, Sassafras scowled and ran under the kitchen table.

"What's wrong, buddy? Remember, this is good bacteria! And you love yogurt!"

Sassafras looked around, but he wouldn't budge.

I shrugged and kept working. As I

finished pouring the mixture of milk and yogurt into the bigger pot of cooling milk, the pot slid a little. Huh. That was weird. It felt like the house had moved.

Mom peered into the pot of cooling milk. "This looks great. I'll just pour this into those last few empty jars and—"

The jars on the kitchen counter rattled.

Mom looked around. "Did you feel that?"

I slowly nodded. Then the kitchen table and chairs shook.

"Earthquake!" Mom shouted.

Mom and I dove under the table. I covered Sassafras with my body and held one arm over the back of my neck and grabbed a table leg. Mom did the same.

The shaking got worse. And then stopped.

Mom and I looked up at each other when the barn doorbell rang.

CHAPTER 2
DOORBELL

The doorbell rang again.

"Should I . . . ?" I asked.

"Hmm. Well, I think it's over," Mom said. "That was unexpected! We never get earthquakes around here. Are you all right?"

"Yeah, I'm fine."

I stayed under the table while Mom stood up and looked around. A glass jar had fallen on the ground and broken.

The doorbell rang again.

"OK, you run out back and see who needs help. Take Sassafras—I don't want him to step on the glass. I'll get this glass cleaned up and finish getting our milk mixture into the cooler to stay warm so we can still have our yogurt tomorrow. I should be there in just a few minutes. And Zoey? If you feel another earthquake, cover up and stay away from anything that could fall on you."

I nodded, and Sassafras and I ran out the door.

By the time we got into the barn, the doorbell had rung two more times. I threw open the back door, stepped out, and almost slammed into a rainbow wall.

Or . . . whoa. Not a wall. A giant, huge, ENORMOUS rainbow *hoof* that filled the entire doorway.

I let out a small squeak.

I looked up, up, up, up, up. And waaaaaay up was a giant horse head with a rainbow mane and . . . a shiny golden

horn?
NO
WAY. A
unicorn?!?!

I cleared
my throat. "Ummm, hello?"

A large booming voice
called out, "HELLO. I HAVE
OW. GIRL HELP?"

It was hurt! I stepped
back and saw that the
ginormous
unicorn was
holding one of its
hooves in the air.
Wait. Was that

what caused the earthquake? If the unicorn was hopping on three legs, then . . .

There was a rustling in the bushes and the smell of peppermint filled the air. I looked toward the bushes as our forest monster friend Gorp popped out.

This was shaping up to be the weirdest day ever.

Gorp calmly walked over to me. "Hey, Zoey. Did you feel that earthquake?"

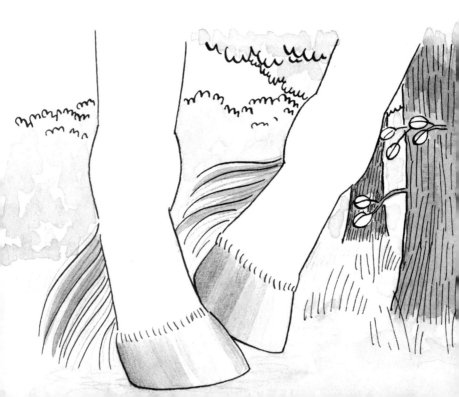

"I . . . uhhh . . . unicorn?" I spluttered.

Gorp looked up at the giant unicorn. "Oh, hey, little one!" Gorp cooed as he pet the enormous unicorn leg.

"Little one?" I thought.

"HELLO MONSTER. HAVE OW."

"Oh, poor thing!" Gorp peered around at the unicorn's raised hoof and nodded. "Aha! That's what caused all that shaking in the forest. Zoey? Are you OK? You're not

saying much."

"So . . . big," I whispered.

"Big?" Gorp chuckled. "But he's so small! He must be a baby."

Wait, what? "But Gorp, he's enormous!"

Gorp looked confused. "How big did you expect him to be?"

I felt my face flush. "I thought unicorns were the same size as horses?"

Gorp laughed really hard. "The size of a horse! Humans are hilarious! Unicorns are always gigantic, obviously." It took him a while to catch his breath. "That was a good one, Zoey."

I realized that Sassafras hadn't thrown himself into Gorp's arms yet. Weird. I looked around for him and was about to call his name when a large, booming voice interrupted me.

"GIRL HELP OW?"

Sassafras would have to wait. "Oh, I'm so sorry!" I hollered up to the unicorn. "Yes, of course. Can you show me the ow?"

CHAPTER 3

FIXING THE OW

The unicorn carefully lowered its gigantic hoof. Gorp and I took a step closer and looked for anything unusual.

I pointed at a scratch about the size of my arm and turned to Gorp. "Do you think that might be causing the trouble?"

Then I heard a squeal behind me. It was my mom. She stood with her hands pressed against her cheeks, staring up at the unicorn. "Oh my goodness! Aren't you just the cutest little thing?" She put her

arm around me. "Oh, Zoey. How special! A little itty-bitty baby unicorn!"

I slapped my forehead. Was I the only one who didn't know the actual size of unicorns?

Gorp cleared his throat.

"Oh my goodness. I didn't see you there, Gorp," Mom said. "How are you doing?" She gave him a hug.

Gorp turned to show off his shiny fur. "Quite well. I was playing with friends in the forest when we felt the earth shaking. They sent me to figure out what it was. I thought you two would know."

The unicorn shifted a little and the ground shook again. "HELP PLEASE?"

"Oh, sorry!" all three of us called up at once.

I pointed to the scratch. "This is all I could find," I told Mom. "It seems pretty small compared to the unicorn's huge leg. Do you think it's like the unicorn version of a paper cut? It's small but it hurts a lot?"

Mom walked around the leg and nodded. "That's all I'm seeing too. What's your plan?"

Oh, right. I needed a plan. I was about to start thinking out loud when my dad opened the back door to our house.

"Honey?" he called. "Why are so many things on the floor in here? Was there an earthquake?"

Mom turned to me. "I'd better go talk to your dad. Good thing he was at the store during this. Since he can't see magical creatures, I am sure he'd be horribly confused right about now! I know you'll come up with a great plan for how to help the unicorn. I'll be inside if you need me."

"GIRL SEE OW? HOW GIRL FIX?"

"I do see the scratch. It must hurt a lot. Let me go grab something and I'll figure out what to do. One minute!" I turned to Gorp. "I'll be right back. I just need to grab my Thinking Goggles to figure this out."

Gorp nodded. "I should head back to my friends. They're still wondering what happened. The baby unicorn will be OK, right?"

"Definitely." I stood up a little straighter. "You can tell your friends I'm taking care of it."

"I will," said Gorp.

"Thanks, Gorp!"

"Oh, and um, say hi to Sassafras for me, I guess." Then he headed back into the forest.

Sassafras! Where was that cat?

I waved goodbye and jogged into the barn. Aha! I found my Thinking Goggles right next to a blanket with a fluffed-up, shaking tail sticking out from under it.

"Sass?" I whispered. I lifted the blanket

and discovered the rest of my fluffed-out, shaking cat. OK, so at least *Sassafras* was also surprised by the unicorn's size.

"Oh, buddy. It's just a baby unicorn. He won't hurt you!" I explained. But it wasn't any use. Sassafras was too freaked out. "Why don't you stay here and I'll go help him?"

"Mrrowww," Sassafras agreed.

I gently covered him up again with the blanket and gave him a reassuring pat. Then I plunked my Thinking Goggles on my head and walked back out to talk to . . . Where were my manners? I'd forgotten to ask if the unicorn had a name.

I leaned my head waaaay back. "Hello again! I've got my Thinking Goggles, so I should have a plan soon. But I forgot to ask—do you have a name?"

The unicorn nodded his gigantic head and a huge gust of wind almost knocked me to the ground. I held on to a nearby tree trunk so I didn't blow away.

"TINY," said the unicorn.

You have got to be kidding me. "Your name is Tiny?"

The unicorn nodded again, and this time my Thinking Goggles flew off.

I chased them down and made a mental note to try to avoid asking Tiny yes or no questions.

"Nice to meet you, Tiny. I'm Zoey. Let's see here. You have a cut on the back of your leg down here."

"ZOEY FIX IT?"

"Yes, I will. I just need to think. Hmmm." I tapped my Thinking Goggles. My knee started to itch. Oh! My knee! I had fallen last week while chasing some friends at school and had gotten a scrape.

"Tiny, when I get a scrape or cut, the first thing my mom asks me to do is rinse it really well with water. Then she dries it and puts some antibacterial cream on it. The cream is like medicine to kill any bad bacteria. After that she covers it with a bandage. In a day or two, I'm as good as new. I'll do the same thing for you, but I need to think bigger. I mean, you're going to need a *slightly* bigger bandage." I giggled, thinking of one of my tiny bandages on Tiny's ginormous unicorn leg.

"OK," said Tiny.

"First up, rinsing. I can't possibly get you to a sink. I need something bigger." I adjusted my Thinking Goggles. "I need a really big faucet like . . . a hose!"

I ran to the side of the barn and

dragged the hose over to Tiny.

Next, I'd have to dry the cut. Mom had dried my knee with a washcloth. Thinking bigger, I realized I'd need a blanket. After drying, I'd need a way to put some antibacterial cream on—a lot of antibacterial cream—and a bandage the size of, well, me. "I'm going inside for

supplies. I'll be right back, Tiny!"

Inside I told my mom the plan, and she distracted my dad while I made a pile on the kitchen table: a blanket, my largest paintbrush, a large tube of antibacterial cream, scissors, and rolls of paper towels, plastic wrap, and packing tape.

I loaded everything in my arms and headed out to Tiny.

"I'm just going to spray some water on your hoof." I held the hose above my head

and rinsed the cut.

"COLD!" Tiny yelped.

"Almost done," I hollered. "I just need to make sure I've washed out any dirt or bad stuff that could be in there."

After one final spray with the hose, I dried his cut with the blanket. Next, I squeezed antibacterial cream onto my paintbrush. I stood on my tippy-toes and painted the whole tube of cream onto the cut. Then I gently placed folded paper towels over the cut. After that I took the plastic wrap and walked in circles around Tiny's leg, pulling the plastic wrap tight to hold the paper towels in place. Finally I topped it all off with some packing tape.

"OK Tiny, I think that should help. Come back tomorrow and I'll check your leg. It should start feeling better really soon."

"ZOEY NICE. THANK YOU."

I moved away from the barn and trees and waved goodbye to Tiny. Then I crouched on the ground and covered my head and neck until Tiny's earth-rattling hops faded away.

CHAPTER 4
WAITING

Sassafras hopped into my lap and looked up at me.

I giggled and tapped his nose. "You missed a spot!"

He licked the dot of yogurt off his nose and settled down, purring in my lap.

The milk mixture we'd warmed overnight had magically changed into yogurt this morning. Well, I guess not *magically*. The bacteria had been working on changing the warm milk into yogurt all

night. But since I couldn't see the bacteria
at work, it did seem a little bit like magic.

I took another bite. "Yummm. These
bacteria are delicious!" I declared.

Mom giggled. "The honey I drizzled on
top doesn't hurt either, huh?"

I smiled and took my last bite. "Do
you think Tiny is OK? It's been raining so
hard."

"Magical creatures tend to heal quickly.

I bet he's feeling much better today."

Sassafras jumped up in surprise and accidentally bonked my chin.

"Ow," I said. "Geez, Sassafras!"

But he wasn't looking at me. He was staring at the door to the backyard. He let out a low growl, then jumped down and huddled under the kitchen table.

"Mom, what's the matter with Sass—" And then I felt it. The house shook. Dishes rattled. Chairs slid. Tiny!

Mom and I dove under the table with Sassafras. I kept my head down with my hand over my neck. I really thought that I'd fixed Tiny's cut. But because our house was shaking so much, I guessed that Tiny wasn't feeling any better.

"But why is Tiny still limping?" I blurted out.

Mom had her head down and neck covered too. "I don't know, sweetie. You'll just have to wait for the doorbell and find

out."

The shaking stopped, and the doorbell rang.

Dad ran into the kitchen. "Are you both OK? What is going on with all of these earthquakes? This is getting out of hand!"

As Mom and I crawled out from under the kitchen table, she squeezed my arm and whispered, "You go. I'll talk to Dad."

Dad kissed my head and hugged Mom. On my way to the door, I heard Mom tell

him that she was having her colleagues look into it. Dad probably thought she meant the professors at the college where she worked, but she really meant me!

I grabbed a raincoat and tugged on my rain boots. Between the rain and the ginormous unicorn, there was no way Sassafras was coming with me.

I ran out to the barn, avoiding the puddles. Once Tiny was better I had plans to do some serious puddle jumping, but right now I needed to work.

Tiny spotted me and took a final hop closer. His good front hoof landed right in an enormous puddle. It created a giant splash of muddy rainwater, which of course completely soaked me.

"OOPS."

I wiped my face and smiled. It's not every day that you get drenched by a giant unicorn. But my smile quickly faded when I saw Tiny still holding the bad leg in the air.

"Hi, Tiny! How is your leg feeling?"
I held my breath, hoping to hear it was
hurting less.

"LEG BAD. OW VERY BAD."

I let out my breath, and my shoulders
drooped. "Can I look?"

Tiny carefully lowered his bad leg, and
I began peeling the tape off. Once I had
unpeeled the tape and the plastic wrap, I

gasped. Tiny's cut looked puffy and red—even worse than it had yesterday.

If it was puffy and red, it meant Tiny's cut was infected. Tiny's leg was only going to get worse and worse. The antibacterial cream had always worked for me. I didn't know what to try next. I took a deep breath and hollered at the top of my lungs.

"MOOOOOOOOOM!!!!"

CHAPTER 5
NOW WHAT?

Mom patted Tiny's hurt leg and shook her head. "You're right, Zoey. The cut is definitely infected. And the antibacterial cream isn't working. What do you think we should do?"

"I don't know." Every time I looked at the horrible cut on Tiny's leg, I felt like crying. It must hurt so much! I wished there was something I could do to fix it. "Wait! Can I go get my Thinking Goggles?"

Mom nodded and I dashed off.

I found them, put them on, adjusted them so they were just right, and headed back to Mom and Tiny. About fifteen seconds after putting on the Thinking Goggles, I figured it out. "An experiment!" I shouted.

Mom smiled.

"I need to get rid of the infection. The antibacterial cream didn't stop the bacteria. I've got to find something that will."

"Good thinking," Mom said, and gestured for me to continue.

"But if I try something else on Tiny's cut, I'll have to wait a day or two to see if it's working. That would take too long." I paced around. "I need to find a way to grow a bunch of the bacteria on my own so I can test different things at the same time. And I also need to figure out a bunch of things that might stop bacteria." I stopped pacing and turned to Mom. "Ummm . . . how do you grow bacteria? And, uhhh, are there other kinds of creams that get rid of it?"

"How about I help you grow the bacteria, and you research other things that will stop it?" Mom suggested.

I nodded. That seemed like it could work.

I called up to Tiny, "I need to set up an

experiment to figure out how to help your cut. Could you maybe lie down out here? I don't want to make you stand for that long. It'll take a while."

I grabbed my Thinking Goggles just before Tiny started nodding, and I managed to keep them on this time.

Mom fixed her hair and then gestured for me to follow her into the barn. "I need your help carrying a few things into the house, and then we'll start cooking."

"Cooking?"

Mom grinned. "You'll see. For now, can you carry this and this?"

She handed me a tall bag of stacked clear and very flat . . . jars? The bag was labeled *Petri Dishes*. Then she handed me a bag of powder labeled *Agar Powder*. Finally she tucked one of her old science journals under her arm.

"Back to the house to get the rest!" she said and waved for me to follow her.

When we got into the house, I set

the petri dishes and agar powder on the kitchen counter, and Mom put out the container of sugar, a big carton of beef broth, and a container of salt.

Sassafras, who'd missed most of the

action by staying inside, paced at our feet and meowed loudly.

I grabbed a chair for him.

Mom flipped open her science journal and slid it toward me. I read the recipe out loud:

Basic Nutrient Agar Recipe

Ingredients: 2½ tsp. sugar
2½ tsp. agar powder
2c. low salt beef broth
2c. water

1. Add all ingredients to a pot. Stir.

2. Heat on medium heat until the mixture begins to boil. Stir to keep the mixture from burning.

3. Once it boils, remove the pot from heat and let it cool for 3 minutes.

4. Pour a thin layer of agar into the bottom section of each petri dish.

5. Allow the agar to set (30 minutes+) before plating bacteria.

★ Remember to store petri dishes with bacteria somewhere warm for fastest results!

"This kind of seems like making yogurt." I skimmed the list of ingredients again. "But way grosser! It's like we're cooking up some sugary-salty-beefy soup."

Mom laughed. "When you make an agar mixture, you're trying to create a place where almost all bacteria will grow. Different kinds of bacteria eat different sorts of things, so this recipe has a little of everything."

She typed something on her laptop, then turned it toward me. The screen was filled with a bunch of photos of those flat jar things—the petri dishes.

"When we made the yogurt, you couldn't see the bacteria, right?" Mom asked.

I shook my head. "Right, it just looked like milk."

"Exactly. It was all mixed up, so it was impossible to see which parts were bacteria. Bacteria are really, really tiny, but when you get enough of them in one place, they make a dot like this." She pointed to a picture on her computer of a polka-dotted petri dish. "The agar mixture will make a really strong gelatin. If you add bacteria on the surface of the cooled agar mixture, instead of mixing it in, it will grow in that one spot. And after a while, if enough of it grows, you can see the dots and know that it's there."

"Coooool!" I scrolled through more pictures on Mom's computer. One had bright orange dots. "Look at that one, Sassafras! It's the same color as you!"

Mom agreed. "But remember, some kinds of bacteria are very dangerous. After we add the bacteria from Tiny's cut to these petri dishes, we'll tape them shut and seal them in a ziplock bag. And no matter how pretty, shiny, smooth, or Sassafras-y the bacteria looks, you should never try to touch it or open a petri dish to get a better look."

"I know. I promise—I won't!"

Mom and I worked together to make the agar recipe from her journal. We heated everything up on the stove so the agar powder dissolved into the stinky soup-like mixture.

"This looks great, Zoey! Can you open all the petri dishes for me? Put one side of each dish onto that cookie sheet, but don't touch the inside. If you do, bacteria from your hands can get in there and grow. We want to keep these clean so we only grow Tiny's bacteria."

I opened all the petri dishes carefully, and Mom slowly poured the hot agar mixture into the halves that were on the cookie sheet. She set a timer for thirty minutes.

"While we wait for these to get solid, can you two grab the box of gloves and the box of cotton swabs from under the bathroom sink?" Mom asked.

Sassafras chattered excitedly when we got back to the kitchen. I gave in and threw him a small handful of cotton swabs. He batted and chased them around the room while we waited.

When the timer went off, Mom moved three of the petri dishes to the kitchen table. "Before we do the real thing, I want you to practice adding the bacteria to the petri dish. It's a little tricky. Remember how I said the cooled agar is like a thick gelatin?"

I nodded. Sassafras bonked into my leg while chasing a runaway cotton swab.

"It's possible to poke through the surface of it. And if you do, it'll be harder to see the bacteria. The first step is to take a cotton swab and rub it gently on Tiny's cut. We'll pretend the table is Tiny's leg for now."

I took a cotton swab and rubbed it really softly on the table.

"Perfect. Now lightly brush it across the

surface of the agar in that first dish."

I tried to, but my cotton swab got stuck in the agar. "Argh!"

"That's OK," said Mom. "Try again."

By the third dish I was able to rub the cotton swab on the surface without poking through the agar.

Sassafras proudly dropped a soggy cotton swab he'd "caught" at my feet. I giggled.

Mom leaned over my shoulder. "Nice work, Zoey! Now it's time to do the real thing."

CHAPTER 6
UNICORN MAGIC

Sassafras decided to be brave and come with Mom and me out back. After all, it was no longer raining, and Tiny was lying down so he seemed a little smaller.

We carefully dodged puddles as we went, but Sassafras slammed to a stop before we got to Tiny. Even lying down, a baby unicorn is pretty enormous.

Poor Tiny looked just awful. I tried not to think about how horrible I'd felt when my ear was infected with bad bacteria. I took a deep breath. This experiment would fix him up.

"Hi, Tiny! We're going to figure out how to heal your infection, but first I need to grow some of the bacteria so I can run experiments. I need to touch your cut, but I'll be very gentle. Is that OK?"

I realized my mistake too late. A yes or no question. Eeek! As Tiny nodded, I held on to my Thinking Goggles, and Mom clutched our supplies tightly, but it was too

late for poor Sassafras. The huge gust of wind rolled him right into a giant puddle. Uh-oh.

For a few seconds, Sassafras sat stunned in the middle of the puddle, soaking wet. Then he hissed, puffed, and jumped all at the same time. He hopped around like crazy trying to shake himself dry.

"Oh, Sassafras!" I put my hands to my cheeks. "I'm so sorry, buddy!"

Tiny watched Sassafras and asked, "CAT HAVE OW?"

"No, he's not hurt. He just really hates being

wet! Don't worry. He'll calm down once he's dry again."

Tiny stretched his neck out toward Sassafras. My poor freaked-out cat was so worried about getting the water off that he didn't see the unicorn horn coming at him.

When Tiny's horn touched Sassafras, a quick burst of rainbow light appeared. When the rainbow light disappeared, it revealed a shocked Sassafras who was completely dry and clean.

"Whoa."

Sassafras picked up and examined each paw. Then he walked around in a circle. "Mrrowww?" he asked.

"TINY FIX OW," Tiny explained.

Sassafras blinked for a moment and then slowly walked over to Tiny. I could tell he was still a little scared, but he gently bopped his head against Tiny's enormous leg and snuggled down next to him and purred.

Then it hit me. "Tiny! You can use your unicorn magic to fix your cut!"

Tiny shook his head, and thankfully it was gentle enough that it didn't blow us away. "HORN NO WORK FOR UNICORNS. HORN FOR OTHERS."

Mom nodded. "I don't think you've seen my journal entries on unicorns yet, Zoey. I've met a few over the years because they are *only* able to help *other* creatures. Their magic doesn't work on other unicorns or themselves. But don't worry,

we'll figure out how to help Tiny."

I stood up straighter. "Yes, we will!"

I grabbed a cotton swab from our
supplies and carefully rubbed it near the
bottom of the cut and tried hard not to
think about how much worse it looked.
Then I rubbed the same cotton swab gently
on the surface of a petri dish. Mom put

the lid on, taped the edges of the dish, and sealed the whole thing in a ziplock bag. I took four different samples from the cut, just to be safe.

I patted Tiny's good leg. "Now we have to wait for the bacteria to grow. Oh! And I need to get started on my research. I've got to make a list of things that I think will get rid of this bacteria!"

Tiny nodded his head so weakly that it only made a gentle breeze.

My heart sank a little. Mom and I hugged Tiny. I ruffled Sassafras's fur and left him behind because he wouldn't budge from Tiny's side.

CHAPTER 7
WHAT WILL WORK?

We had to let this bacteria grow in a warm place, just like the yogurt. So we used the same cooler as our incubator. Mom just refilled the glass jars with new hot water. I snuggled the four ziplock bags with the petri dishes down between the jars and made sure they were nice and toasty warm. Mom threw all of our used supplies into the garbage, and we both washed our hands really well.

"It will take a while for the bacteria to

grow, right?"

"Well, normally, yes, it usually takes one or two days to be able to see bacteria on a petri dish. But magical things always seem to grow more quickly than normal things. I think we'll have an answer in a few hours."

"Oh, that's awesome! While we wait, I need to figure out what I'm going to use against the bacteria in the second experiment." I tapped my Thinking Goggles. Nothing. I started walking around the kitchen. When I got near the kitchen counter, I tapped my hand along it. I reached the kitchen sink and spotted the soap. "OH! Soap!" I exclaimed.

"Good," Mom replied.

"OK, one idea down, a few more to go." I shifted my Thinking Goggles again. For some reason I felt like walking backward. So I did. I ended up at the edge of the kitchen counter right by a container of disinfecting wipes my mom used to clean the counters. "WIPES!" I shouted triumphantly.

"Another great idea. What else?"

I took one more lap around the kitchen. I started rubbing my hands together. Wait a minute. "Hey, doesn't Sophie's mom use some kind of hand sanitizer made from plants to get rid of the bacteria on our hands before we eat? Oooh! Are there plants that might stop the bacteria?"

"Yes, there are! Excellent work! The soap and wipes are pretty straightforward. But you'll probably want to do some reading to figure out which plants to use. I have just the book for you." Mom went to her office and came back with a big plant book.

"Before we had antibiotics, like you took for your ear infection, or antibacterial cream, like we use on your cuts and scrapes, people used plants to treat infected cuts. You can read about lots of them in here. Let me know what you decide to try."

After I'd read for a while, I grabbed my science journal. There were so many plants to choose from! I decided to pick only the plants I knew I could find at our house. Once I had a list of four plant options, I leapt to my feet.

"I have a plan!" I announced. No one was in the kitchen to hear me, but I was still excited. I flipped to a new page in my science journal.

QUESTION: What will get rid of Tiny's bacteria?

But I couldn't concentrate. I gathered up everything and headed outside. I needed to talk it through with Sassafras.

Tiny was awake this time, but he sure seemed like he felt terrible. His eyes were a little puffy and he barely held his head off the ground. Sassafras was curled up by Tiny's chin, but he looked up when I walked over.

"I have a plan," I reassured them. After snuggling them both, I settled down cross-legged on the ground by Tiny's head. I opened my science journal and picked up where I left off.

"OK, let's see here—what's my hypothesis? I mean, I guess soap or the disinfecting wipes could get rid of the

bacteria. But Tiny's from the forest, so using a plant sort of makes sense to me. Of all the plants on my list, onions seem the most powerful—they always make my nose wrinkle and my eyes water, so I think they'll be the best at stopping this bacteria."

HYPOTHESIS: I think onion will get rid of Tiny's bacteria.

"Materiaallls," I sang.

MATERIALS: Petri dishes, agar mixture, cotton swabs, ziplock bags, Tiny's bacteria, garlic, onion, oregano, thyme, soap, disinfecting wipes, marker, tape, spoons.

Mom came out to the backyard. "How's it going?"

I proudly handed her my science journal and hopped up. "I'm going to check on the petri dishes!" I dashed into the house and peeked in the cooler.

"Nothing yet," I announced when I came back out.

"Your plan looks good." Mom handed me my science journal. "Why don't you hang out here with Tiny and Sassafras? I'll call you when it's time to check the bacteria again."

"Thanks, Mom!" I said and snuggled up next to two of my favorite animals.

CHAPTER 8
STUMPED

Tiny was not doing well. I brushed his tail with one of our rakes, and that seemed to make him feel a little better. But what Tiny really needed was a fixed leg. It felt like I had been waiting in the yard for hours when my mom finally called me in.

I ran to the cooler and opened the lid, excited to move on to the second part of my experiment.

"But . . . ?" I looked up at my mom. "The bacteria should've grown by now, right?"

Mom glanced at the clock. "I really thought it would have."

"So, what does this mean?"

She sat down at the kitchen table. "Well, maybe the bacteria just needs more time to grow. Or maybe the agar mixture is missing something this bacteria requires. I'm not sure which."

I sat down next to Mom and flumped my head on my arms. "We really need to figure this out! I don't want to waste any more time."

Mom rubbed my back. "I know what you mean."

"Can we make a new agar mixture while we give this one more time to grow?"

Mom nodded. "Let's try it. But what do you want to add this time?"

I got up and paced and tapped my goggles. "Come on, Thinking Goggles! Give me some ideas," I muttered under my breath.

But instead of new ingredients, all I could think about was yogurt. Was this really the best time for a snack?

"ARGH!" I pouted. "The only thought I'm having is about yogurt. I don't want to eat! I want to solve this . . . OH!"

Mom raised an eyebrow.

"Oh! Oh!" I said again. "Yogurt! Of course!"

"Care to share those thoughts?" Mom asked.

"Well, we knew we could grow the store-bought yogurt bacteria in milk, because the bacteria was already growing there."

"Right," Mom said.

"We know that bacteria on Tiny grows on unicorns, so we just need to find a way to add some unicorn . . . something . . . to the agar mixture!"

"Ooh, great thinking, Zoey! That just might work. What are you thinking of adding?"

"Well, the cut on Tiny's leg is in his fur. Maybe I could clip some fur from one of his good legs and we could mix that in?"

"Excellent plan. You grab the fur and I'll start cooking a new batch."

In no time at all, Mom and I had petri dishes filled with new agar—now with unicorn-ness added! Once they cooled, I took them out, and with my gloves and cotton swabs, I carefully added bacteria from Tiny's cut to the new petri dishes. Mom refilled the jars in the cooler with more hot water, and I gently settled the new petri dishes next to the old ones.

"The old petri dishes still have nothing on them," I told Mom as I closed the lid.

"Let's hope the new ones are more effective," she said.

I sat down at the kitchen table. "And now we wait."

CHAPTER 9
WHOA

After what seemed like forever, but was actually only about three hours, Mom said I could take a peek in the cooler.

"But don't be disappointed if there's no bacteria yet," she reminded me.

I squinched my eyes closed, made a silent wish, and then opened the cooler. "WHOAAAAA."

Mom squished in right beside me.

"Whooooaaa," she said.

For a full minute we just stared. The

new petri dishes were covered with shiny
red dots that glowed red. It was pretty . . .
and also kind of creepy.

"ACK! I'm wasting time!" I said,
bouncing on my toes. "I need to get started
on my second experiment NOW!"

"How can I help?" Mom asked.

"Can you start another batch?" I asked.
"I'll get some more unicorn fur and grab

the onions, garlic, oregano, and thyme from our garden."

"Let's make it happen!" Mom said, turning to the stove.

I ran out the back door. Tiny was sleeping and Sassafras paced around him. I quickly clipped some fur. I figured Tiny wouldn't mind, and I didn't want to wake him.

Next I ran to the garden. While I worked, Sassafras chattered at me and kept

glancing back at Tiny. I could tell from how upset he was that Tiny was getting worse. "Don't worry, Sassafras. We're hurrying!" I promised. I kissed his head and dashed back to the house with my supplies.

I burst into the kitchen. "Tiny's getting worse, Mom. Sassafras is really upset!"

Mom frowned. "I know, baby. But we're doing everything we can. The agar mixture is ready. What next?"

"I'll wash all the plants. After that, I think chopping them up will help them mix into the agar. It'll also make them easier to measure. Can you get the food chopper out for me?"

Mom helped me chop the onion, garlic, oregano, and thyme. I added the soap and disinfecting wipes to the lineup and grabbed a tablespoon to measure each ingredient to add to the petri dishes.

"Wait!" Mom slid a permanent marker toward me. "Don't forget to label them."

"That was a close one! Thanks, Mom." I labeled each of the seven dishes:

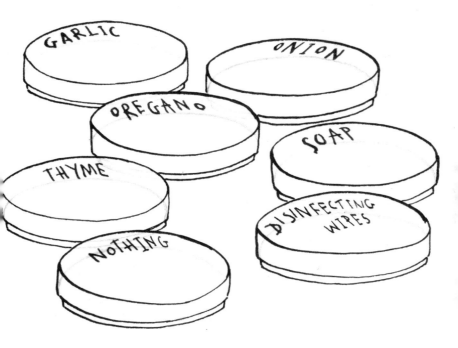

After they were labeled, I spooned a tablespoon of each ingredient into the correctly labeled dish, washing my spoon in between each ingredient. For the dish with the disinfecting wipes, I decided to add a tablespoon of the liquid from the bottom of the container.

I left one dish with nothing added. I needed to see how much bacteria grew without anything there. If any of the petri dishes with an added ingredient grew less bacteria, then I'd know that ingredient was working.

Mom carefully poured the same amount of hot agar mixture into each of the petri dishes. I used a clean spoon to stir each ingredient in, and we left them to

cool.

We both paced the kitchen as we waited for the timer to let us know that the agar had cooled and was ready for the next step. When it buzzed, we jumped, then grabbed all the supplies and ran to the backyard.

Tiny's cut was even more red and swollen than just a few hours earlier. I had to take a few breaths so I didn't start crying. This experiment had to work.

He must have been feeling really awful because he kept sleeping as I used the cotton swab to get bacteria to put on the new petri dishes. Mom sealed them all up and handed the ziplock bags to me.

I took the ziplock bags inside the house and put them in the cooler while Mom added new hot water to the jars. We then washed our hands and tapped our legs nervously as we sat waiting.

"Hey, why don't you write down your procedure while we wait," Mom suggested.

PROCEDURE:

1. Label seven petri dishes.
2. Add nothing to dish labeled "nothing."
3. Add one tablespoon of each ingredient to the correctly labeled dish (Use a clean spoon each time).
4. Pour the same amount of agar mixed with unicorn fur into each dish.
5. Stir each dish with a clean spoon.
6. Wait 30 minutes for the agar to cool.
7. Add bacteria to each dish using a cotton swab.
8. Seal dishes with tape, and put into ziplock bags.
9. Place in a cooler filled with jars of hot water (To keep pet dishes warm).

"Good idea," I said and got to work.

"Do you think it's time yet?" I asked Mom.

"I'm not sure it's been long enough, but it won't hurt to check."

We both walked over to the cooler. I held my breath as we opened it.

"YESSSSSSS!" we cheered at the same time. We had an answer.

CHAPTER 10
TWO ANSWERS

We had two answers, actually. "Look!" I held up two petri dishes. "Both onion and garlic worked!"

"Wonderful!" exclaimed Mom.

I took a closer look at the petri dishes. "Hmmm, it looks like there's just a little bit of bacteria on the one with onion. But it's a really small amount." Next I looked at the garlic petri dish. "OK, there's seriously nothing on this one. Does that make garlic the best choice?"

"You got it." Mom smiled.

"So now we need a LOT of garlic. Like maybe *all* of our garlic?" My dad was obsessed with garlic so we had two full rows of it growing in our backyard. But that cut on Tiny was huge. I was going to need all of it. "Do you think Dad will mind?"

"We'll have to come up with something to tell Dad," Mom said. "But I know if he could see Tiny, he would absolutely give up his garlic."

That settled it. With Tiny getting worse, I didn't want to waste a single moment. I threw on my shoes and grabbed a bucket from outside the kitchen door.

Tiny's droopy eyes were barely open. Sassafras perked up when he saw me burst out the back door. "We figured out how to fix the cut!" I shouted across the yard to them. I bolted to the garden, where I probably set a new record for the fastest garlic-harvesting ever.

Mom and I set up a production line where I washed the garlic and she chopped off the roots and stems. I chopped batch after batch of garlic. Our kitchen smelled like an Italian restaurant!

I grabbed all my supplies for a new bandage for Tiny. Mom helped me carry those and the big old bowl of chopped garlic outside.

We set it all down, and Sassafras

trotted toward the bowl. He took one sniff, wrinkled his nose, and sneezed.

I walked over to Tiny and gently pet his nose. "OK, Tiny. I think we've got this figured out. I ran an experiment, and garlic got rid of the bad bacteria from your cut. I've chopped up a big bowl of garlic, and I'm going to gently cover your cut with it. Then I'll bandage it up like I did before. Your cut should feel better in a few hours."

I gave his nose a pet. "I know you aren't feeling very well, but it will be easiest for me to get the garlic and the bandage on if you are standing. Do you think you can stand up for me?"

Tiny gave a very small nod. But it barely ruffled my hair. Oh, Tiny!

It took him a minute, but Tiny finally stood up to his full height. He carefully set his bad leg down so I could reach the swollen cut easily.

"First, I'm using a clean paintbrush to spread the chopped garlic on your cut. It might tickle!"

Tiny wiggled a little but did a good job holding pretty still.

"Now I'm going to cover the wound and the garlic with the paper towels. Mom, can you hold this while I wrap it?" Mom held the paper towels in place with both hands while I walked around Tiny's huge leg, pulling the plastic wrap snug. Finally I used the packing tape to keep it all in the right spot on Tiny's tree trunk of a leg.

I patted him. "All set, Tiny! You can hang out here if you'd like. I'm sure Sassafras would love to keep you company."

"TINY FAMILY WORRY. TINY SHOULD GO."

"Oh, right. That makes sense." I was a little bummed to see him go, but I knew how my parents would worry if I were gone for this long. Especially if I were sick!

Mom and I hunkered down as Tiny

began his earth-rattling hops back into the forest, but Sassafras took off after Tiny.

"Come back, Sassafras! You can't follow Tiny!" I hollered.

Sassafras completely ignored me. Stinker.

Luckily, Tiny turned around. "NO KITTY. NO FOLLOW. TINY BE BACK SOON."

Sassafras grumbled and reluctantly made his way back to us. Tiny had just disappeared when Dad burst from the house.

"Another earthquake? This is getting out of hand! Are you all OK?"

Whoops. Dad was home from work! Mom jogged over and put her arm around him. I saw him slowly relax as they went back inside. Whatever she was saying to him was working!

I made a silent wish that Tiny was already starting to feel better, and then headed inside for dinner.

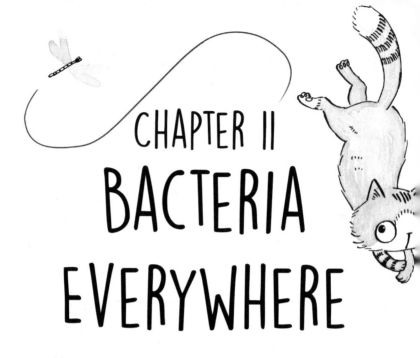

CHAPTER 11
BACTERIA
EVERYWHERE

The next morning Sassafras and I woke up super early. We spent almost a full hour with our noses pressed to the window, looking for any sign of Tiny, until Mom

suggested that we keep busy while we wait.

First, I updated my science journal:

RESULTS:

Petri dish	How much bacteria
Nothing	a lot
Soap	a lot.
Disinfecting wipes	a lot.
onion	Just 2 small ~~dots~~.
garlic	NONE!!YAY!!!
thyme	a little less than the nothing dish
oregano	a little less than the nothing dish

CONCLUSION:
Garlic works the best at getting rid of this unicorn bacteria.

I finished that. Still no Tiny.

So then Mom and I cooked up a new batch of agar mixture without unicorn hair, and she gave me a whole bunch of cotton swabs to explore the house.

I took samples from my face, Sassafras's mouth, the bottoms of my shoes, the bottoms of Sassafras's paws, the bathroom and kitchen sinks, the front doorknob, my bedroom doorknob, and under my fingernails.

"Ooooh, these are going to be so gross!" I giggled in anticipation.

I was just filling the last of the glass jars with hot water to warm up the cooler when Sassafras hopped up on the kitchen counter.

"Sass! Down! You know you're not supposed to be up here!"

Sassafras not only ignored me but also started purring really loudly. He was staring out the window.

"No way!" I squealed. Our whole backyard was lit up by a giant rainbow.

Sassafras and I both ran for the back door and burst into the yard. Rainbow light was everywhere. It was like some kind of amazing dream!

"TINY!" I yelped in delight.
"MRROOOOOWWW!" cried Sassafras.
We both bounded over to Tiny who
stood on all four legs! He was positively

glowing. He looked incredible!

"ZOEY LIKE A UNICORN! ZOEY FIXED OW!" Tiny declared.

I ran to the bandage and peeled it off. There was just a pale pink line where the swollen, angry cut had been just yesterday. "Hooray for garlic!" I cheered.

I felt a hand on my shoulder and turned to see Mom. "You did it, sweetie! Well done." She held my camera out to me.

"Mom, you're a genius!" Now that Tiny felt better, it was the perfect time to ask for a photo. I always try to get a photo of the magical creatures I help to add to my science journal so I can remember them. Photos of magical creatures are the coolest because some of the magic stays behind in the photo.

"Tiny?" I called up. "If it's OK to take a photo with you, would you put your head down by me?" I felt clever for thinking of a way to ask that wouldn't involve Tiny nodding and blowing us all over.

Tiny put his head down low, and I gave his velvety nose a big hug.

Mom snapped a photo. "Got it!"

"Can you stay and play with me and Sassafras, Tiny?"

"SORRY ZOEY. TINY NEED GO HOME. TINY GONE LONG TIME. THANK YOU ZOEY FOR HELP OW."

Tiny bent his head low again and nuzzled each of our cheeks. Sassafras purred super loudly again.

Just then, my dad raced into the backyard. "What is going on?" He looked around and rubbed his eyes. "First we have earthquakes, and now there's an enormous rainbow in our backyard?"

He came toward us and stood just inches from Tiny's hoof. But of course he had no idea, because he couldn't see Tiny. "It's the craziest thing I've ever seen," he said, looking through the ginormous unicorn and around at the rainbow-filled yard.

Mom and I covered our mouths with our hands to keep from bursting out laughing. If only Dad knew he was standing at the foot of a giant unicorn.

While Dad took another look around the yard, Mom and I secretly waved to Tiny.

Tiny gave us one last "BYE-BYE," then gracefully and silently galloped into the forest.

Mom slid the photo into my hand and walked Dad back inside as he scratched his head.

Sassafras was pretty bummed. I thought a tuna treat might cheer him up. When I set the bowl of tuna on the ground, I gave him a big hug. "You did such a good job taking care of Tiny."

He bumped his head into my leg and took a huge bite of tuna. Once the purring started, I knew he'd be OK.

I looked down at my photo and tilted it this way and that. The rainbow that had filled our whole yard shimmered, and Tiny sparkled. I couldn't help but smile.

I added the photo of Tiny to my science journal, took one last look, then turned my journal to a new page. A new page that was blank and ready for the next magical creature we would meet.

GLOSSARY

Agar: A gelatin-like substance. If you mix it with other ingredients and pour the mixture into a petri dish to cool, you can grow bacteria on it!

Antibiotic: Medicine that gets rid of bacteria (your doctor might give you an antibiotic if you are sick with a bacterial infection).

Bacteria: Tiny microscopic living things that can be harmful or helpful, depending on the type.

Disinfectant: A substance, like bleach or soap, that gets rid of bacteria and viruses.

Infection: When harmful bacteria or viruses get inside your body and make you sick.

Petri dish: A container that scientists use to grow bacteria in.

ABOUT THE AUTHOR
AND ILLUSTRATOR

ASIA CITRO used to be a science teacher, but now she plays at home with her two kids and writes books. When she was little, she had a cat just like Sassafras. He loved to eat bugs and always made her laugh (his favorite toy was a plastic human nose that he carried everywhere). Asia has also written three activity books: *150+ Screen-Free Activities for Kids, The Curious Kid's Science Book,* and *A Little Bit of Dirt.* She has yet to find a baby dragon in her backyard, but she always keeps an eye out, just in case.

MARION LINDSAY is a children's book illustrator who loves stories and knows a good one when she reads it. She likes to draw anything and everything but does spend a completely unfair amount of time drawing cats. Sometimes she has to draw dogs just to make up for it. She illustrates picture books and chapter books as well as painting paintings and designing patterns. Like Asia, Marion is always on the lookout for dragons and sometimes thinks there might be a small one living in the airing cupboard.

for activities and more visit
ZOEYANDSASSAFRAS.COM